With an Everlasting Love

KAY ARTHUR

HARVEST HOUSE PUBLISHERS
Eugene, Oregon 97402

WITH AN EVERLASTING LOVE
Copyright © 1995 by Kay Arthur
Published by Harvest House Publishers
Eugene, Oregon 97402

Library of Congress Cataloging-in-Publication Data

Arthur, Kay, 1933–
    With an everlasting love / Kay Arthur.
        p.   cm.
    ISBN 1-56507-279-0
    I. Title.
    PS3551.R764W58   1994
    813'.54—dc20
                                                            94-26418
                                                                CIP
                                                                AC

Printed in the United States of America

95   96   97   98   99   00   01   /   10   9   8   7   6   5   4   3   2

With an Everlasting Love

Put me like a seal over your heart
Like a seal on your arm.
For love is as strong as death'
Jealousy is as severe as Sheol;
Its flashes are flashes of fire,
The very flame of the Lord.

Song of Solomon 8:6

CHAPTER ONE

"**A**ny Jew who has not a wife is no man." It was written in the Talmud. That settled it. The time had come for his son Joshua to take a wife. There could be no more delay. Shaddai paced the floor, saying these things aloud to himself, as he awaited Joshua's return.

Although the sound of his words was at times lost in his beard, anyone who observed him would have known that whatever this patriarch was saying, he meant. Determination was engraved in furrows of concern upon the aged parchment of his face.

His reasoning continued. "My son has already reached manhood. Why, a marriage contract should have been made long ago! I am old! I need grand-children. Besides, if Joshua does not marry, then who will carry on my name? Only one son, that's all

I have . . . only one, my Joshua. Ah, Joshua, what a son you are!"

With that thought, Shaddai's pacing came to an abrupt halt. Suddenly a smile illuminated his face, dispelling the clouds of determination. Thoughts of his son always brought smiles, for although Shaddai had only one child, there was no child that could equal Joshua. Even the men who sat with Shaddai at the city gates would concur. No one debated him or even raised a quizzical eyebrow when he would say, "If all the sons of Israel were mine, they could not equal my Joshua. He is my son, my only begotten son with whom I am well pleased."

Each time he said it, no matter how often, they could only nod their heads in assent, for they, too, would have been well pleased had Joshua been their son. Impeccable in character, endowed with great wisdom, perfect in obedience, he was a son who always and only did those things which pleased his father. Oh, yes, Shaddai was a father to be envied, and he knew it!

"Maybe that is why I have been so slow to follow my Jewish traditions. I cannot choose a bride for Joshua without his consent! Why, how could I ever find a woman suitable for one such as Joshua!"

That thought started Shaddai pacing again as he mentally began a journey through the streets and families of his city. He had to find a bride for Joshua! Sensing the urgency of his plight, he paced more rapidly, halting abruptly each time the name of some young virgin would come to mind. Yet each name only brought a negative shake of the head, and the pacing would begin again. In his mind's eye, Shaddai stopped at the door of every fine family who had a virgin daughter. Yet every time he would shake his head, "No!" with such vigor that his beard would swing like a pendulum from shoulder to shoulder.

Having exhausted every suitable home in his city, Shaddai remembered how he had discussed this very problem with the men at the gate. Every one of those men would like to have the honor of having Joshua as a son-in-law. Not only would the fortunate father gain much honor for his daughter, but what a dowry he would receive also! No one in the city was wealthier than Shaddai. No one was more genuinely admired than this father and son. Their lives bore a righteousness none could question, not even those who might be jealous. Maybe this was why not one of the city fathers could recommend his daughter nor any other virgin he knew. Who could measure up to Joshua? Who could live in the home of Shaddai and bear his name and his son's sons? The problem of a bride for Joshua had been discussed often, yet even as the men considered other daughters of Israel from other cities, they could not think of a truly suitable bride. Often the men would shake their heads and say, "How could imperfection be married to perfection?"

Suddenly Shaddai's troubled reverie was broken. "Father! Father, I'm home. Where are you?"

"Here, my son, at my writing table." With that, Shaddai sat down, almost as if to relieve himself of the burden he had been carrying.

"Abba! What are those furrows on your face? What is troubling you?"

"Abba" was Joshua's term of endearment for his father, held over from childhood and used whenever he sensed his father was burdened by some concern.

Smiling, Shaddai stood to his feet and opened his arms wide to embrace his son. As Joshua's arms locked behind his father, he gave him his usual squeeze. This time, however, instead of dropping his arms to his side, Joshua stepped back an arm's length and put both hands on Shaddai's shoulders.

Looking full in his father's beloved face, he said, "Something is on your mind. What is it?" They never kept any secrets from one another, thus Joshua knew that all he need do was ask.

"It is a bride for you, my son. You must have a bride. We can delay no longer."

"Fine. I agree. Yet—"

"Where shall we ever find a woman suitable to be your bride?" his father interrupted. "I know of none!"

"Father," the word came gently, enshrouded with peace. "Father, I have found a bride. When I tell you all about her, I know you will concur, for I know your heart as well as mine. Come. Let us have some refreshment, and I will tell you all that is on my heart."

Father and son sat for hours in the courtyard, talking intently. Finally, when the heavens above dimmed their lights, signaling the end of another day, Shaddai gingerly rose from his seat. Stiff from sitting so long, he placed his hands upon his knees as if to unlock his joints. Then moving with caution, he slowly straightened out to his full stature.

Stretching his arms up toward the star-studded heavens, he said, "Now, my son, I have listened carefully to all your reasoning and requests. What a son you are! It is almost as if I live in your skin, for our thoughts are so much the same! Christianna was upon my heart also. There is such potential in that young woman. Yet who would see it? Who has seen it? No one! No, because of her mixed blood, Jew and Gentile, and because of her low estate, none has looked past the circumstances of her life to see the potential of that precious soul. It is all buried under the rubble of her life."

Shaddai was filled with anticipation as he began to wax eloquent. "Ah, but let a little excavation be done. Let rubble be carried off. Let her be loved unconditionally. She shall rise as magnificent as the walls of Jerusalem. She shall blossom like the rose of Sharon. Like a lily among the thorns, so your darling shall be among the maidens." Then, like a resounding crescendo, came his blessing. "Son, I heartily concur."

For a brief moment the glint from the oil lamp on the table caught Joshua's joyful smile. Shaddai could not see his son's dark brown eyes in the darkness of the night, but he was sure they must be twinkling along with the stars in the heavens.

"And, Father, although we will break custom a little, do you concur with my betrothal plans also?"

"Yes! Yes!" Excitement rang in Shaddai's voice. "They are perfect! Perfectly suited for the bride-to-be and for a situation such as hers. Why, if you did not woo her first, if you did not give her a sense of worth, she might never know that to you she is beloved even though others see nothing lovely about her." Shaddai's voice began to raise in adamancy, as he said, "She must know she is loved and precious in your sight before she ever agrees to the betrothal. When she enters into our marriage covenant, she must be convinced that this marriage had its roots in love, not in convenience or in the fleeting passion of desire." Joshua smiled at his father's "our." Oh, the security of knowing you are loved first, loved unconditionally!

"It's settled then, Father? We will have Eliezer deliver my letters to her periodically?" Joshua paused. It seemed important to him that his plans be confirmed once more, step by step.

"But, of course, Son. As you said, Christianna would never dream you could ever want her. And besides, if she did, surely the people of her city would convince her that she would never measure up to being your wife and my daughter. For although they have never seen you in that city, your reputation has preceded you. No, we shall do as you have planned. You write the letters; Eliezer can deliver them. The journey will not be too great for him. Besides, you know how he loves to travel. Then when we are certain that Christianna is duly informed and convinced of your love, when you have thoroughly explained to her all the responsibilities of being your wife, and when we think she understands the depth of what it means to commit herself to your loving lordship, then Eliezer can present the marriage contract and tell her what price you are willing to pay for her. That marriage contract, that *kesubah*, will give her all the security she needs. I know she will not refuse."

"But, Father, remember," Joshua's words were covered with concern as he sought understanding, "remember, she cannot see me until the night of our wedding. Eliezer must make all the arrangements. Christianna must be willing to marry me without seeing me. Her decision must be made on the basis of what she knows about me and of what she knows of our life together. It cannot be because of the way I look, or because of the way she feels when I touch her, or even because of what I can do for her. Her commitment must be a solid commitment to the mode of life she will live as my wife. I must—" Joshua paused, for a tremor had caught his voice. As if an unexpected chill had suddenly caused him to shake, his words came forth trembling, yet anchored in determination. "I must have a wife who will be one with me, Father. Even as we are one."

Shaddai walked to the table where Joshua was still sitting. Then reaching down with his right hand, he turned Joshua's face upward toward his and said, "My beloved son, I understand. One as we are one. Right now, where she is as a person, it seems impossible. But remember that with your father nothing is impossible. All things are possible with me, and so it shall be. I love you, my son, and I will show you all that you should do. Speak as I have taught you. Do nothing on your own initiative, and it shall come to pass. I know the prayer of your heart. Someday you and Christianna will be one, and the glory I have given you I will bestow on her also."

CHAPTER TWO

Christianna knew nothing of the plans that were being made for her. Joshua had seen Christianna, but she had never seen him. Even in her dream of dreams she would not have imagined that she, Christianna, would have the opportunity to become the wife of the son of Shaddai. Like all women, Christianna thought much about love. And yet she had never even begun to comprehend that such a great love could someday be bestowed upon her. Why, at that point in her life, all that she had heard of Joshua and Shaddai were rumors, illusions . . . or were they distortions? Who knew the truth about them anyway, and who cared? Their lives would never touch hers; they were worlds apart. Hers seemed a hell. From what she had heard, theirs seemed like heaven. And heaven and hell would be separated for eternity. As far as Christianna was concerned, Shaddai and Joshua might even have been myths—characters from some tall story told by one journeyman to another.

Life was hard for Christianna. She felt like a slave, a slave of passion. It had been her parents' passion that had made her a despised half-breed, carrying both Jewish and Gentile blood. To which culture did she belong? Jews wouldn't have a thing to do with Gentiles and vice versa. Each despised the other, and Christianna despised herself. And that made her angry, for she was also a slave of her own passions. Oh, she had retained her virginity. Those passions were in control because Christianna couldn't begin to fathom any decent man desiring a half-breed who came from a family such as hers. They were poor and they were despised. And although some thought Christianna comely in looks, she had determined that she would not be a cast-off vessel of some man's passing pleasure. Besides, what father of Israel would seek her for his son? None. And what Gentile would want a half-breed Jewess, except for a night or two?

No, Christianna's passions were deeper than her sexual drive, and, therefore, they were passions not as easily satisfied. Christianna longed for, craved, another life. She wished that she could go back and crawl up into another womb. She wished she could be born again of other parents in other circumstances. She dreamed of how life might have been, and it made her mad. Mad! Angry! Frustrated! For her life would never be different.

How often she thought of Solomon's words from the old scrolls: "Exactly as a man is born, thus will he die. So what is the advantage to him who toils for the wind?" To which words Christianna would bitterly reply, "Naked I came into this world, naked I shall return, and naked shall I remain all my life . . . to be looked upon, pitied, despised, but not helped, not changed. Nothing will ever change. I simply toil for the wind." She faced the fact that as she had been born, so she would die. Yet facing the facts did not change the longing of her heart. Almost daily the passion to be different, to start again, would well up inside her until she thought she would go mad. Over and over she would muse, *Why, oh, why can't I be like others, content with life on a lower plane? How much easier it would be to live without this longing.*

And it would have been. Yet to live without longing is to become apathetic. And apathetic was one thing Christianna was not. There was a scrappiness about her, like the yellow dog that lived in her village. No one seemed to care about him. In fact, he bore the brunt of their bad humor. Yet the mutt was determined he was going to survive. Maybe that was why Christianna always tucked a scrap of meat or bread in her pocket whenever she ventured to the marketplace. Dog or not, their lives were much alike.

CHAPTER THREE

T he barking grew louder as Christianna
approached the market. Funny, she thought, it
sounds like ol' Cur, yet he doesn't sound angry.
Strange . . . he sounds excited. But what could excite that
mongrel? Has he not seen it all already, roaming and
exploring every cranny of this village?

Christianna quickened her steps. No one was
going to torment ol' Cur if she could help it. She
jumped up onto the stone step of one of the shops,
straining her neck to get a full view of the marketplace. But she could see nothing. Cur—or some
dog—seemed to be the center of attraction and the
source of amusement for the crowd which blocked
her view.

Murmuring excuses and apologies, Christianna
determinedly moved through the crowd until she
finally broke through the wall of people. At her
arrival, people burst forth in laughter. Stunned at

---

first, thinking they were laughing at her, she took several steps backward.

Then, looking up, Christianna saw the reason for their sudden outburst. There was Cur, his head cocked to one side, looking at a man sprawled flat on his back right there in the middle of the marketplace. Shocked by the sudden outburst of laughter, Cur looked from side to side. Then, sensing that the arena was all his, he again took up his barking, dashing back and forth from the man to the perimeter of this human arena. Sensing man's approval for the first time, Cur was in his glory. Excited, he threw himself in full motion, running around and around his circle of admirers. After stopping once again and cocking his head, he ran straight for the man who was now sitting up convulsing with laughter.

What a delightful man! thought Christianna. Cur must have thought so, too, for he wanted to play some more. Snatching the sleeve of the man's robe, he gently resumed his tug-of-war. Now Christianna understood how the man came to be on the ground. Apparently Cur in his enthusiasm had tugged on the man's robe, caught him off balance, and landed him in the dirt. Growling playfully and tugging at the man's sleeve, Cur once again cocked his head, looked at the crowd, dropped the sleeve, and then suddenly leaped, landing on all fours in the man's lap! As he did so, his two front paws once again flattened the man to the ground.

As Cur stood on top of the man, affectionately licking away his salty tears of laughter, Christianna tried to regain her composure. Someone had to come to this poor man's rescue. Oblivious to the crowd and feeling as if she were responsible for the animal, Christianna moved into the center of the marketplace, dangling the meat she had brought in her outstretched hand.

"Cur! Cur! You scoundrel, come here! Leave that poor man alone. Here! Come! Get this morsel." It was hard to suppress her laughter and speak with authority. Perhaps it was the playfulness of her voice that finally caused Cur to abandon his perch atop the man and come to Christianna, for the food didn't seem to entice him that much. Either Cur had eaten a hearty lunch, or he had found the loving approval of man more important than food.

The fun over, the crowd began to disperse. Yet among all there was a sense of camaraderie because of the whole incident. They had shared something in common, something that had delighted them. Even Cur was looked upon in a new light. But it was the man who caused the most discussion, for he was the one who had started it all by patting Cur and then playing tug-of-war with him. As the people walked away, they discussed the man's unusual behavior. Jewish men didn't ordinarily play with stray dogs. Dogs were, for the most part, treated cruelly in Israel.

"Who is he anyway?" they were asking.

"Don't know. Doesn't belong to this village," others said.

"His robe's a fine one. Fine donkey, too. Wonder what he's doing here?"

The object of their queries and speculation rose to his feet, brushed the dust from his robe, and smiled from ear to ear. "Thanks for rescuing me," he said to Christianna. "Is that your dog?"

Normally Christianna would have been offended, for dogs like Cur were despised, and no real lady would ever lay claim to such a creature. Yet looking at his countenance, she knew this man was without guile. "No, it's not my dog. He's a stray. But I like him. He's a survivor, and, as you can see, he has personality."

Christianna's response was free and natural, and the man noticed it. Gone was the usual propriety that bid her as a woman to be reserved in carrying on a conversation with a man she did not know. The man looked at her and smiled. He liked this young maiden. Talking with her would not be too unseemly, for since she was not veiled, he knew she was not betrothed. "I'm Eliezer of the house of Shaddai in Jerusalem," he said.

Christianna's smile ended as her mouth dropped open. "So it is true. There is a Shaddai," she mused. But would the wealthy, awesome Shaddai she had heard of have a servant such as this! One so real, so gentle and kind, yet with such a sense of humor?

Eliezer took in her whole countenance—the drop of her mouth, the ensuing silence, her eyes lighting with recognition . . . or was it query? "You know of my master?"

"Just hearsay," said Christianna, trying to keep the curiosity out of her voice. "And of that, precious little. I do not move in a culture such as his. I come from a different world."

Her openness amazed Eliezer, even as he sensed a hint of bitter longing in her voice. "And what is your name? May I know so that I might address you properly?"

There was no brashness, only candidness, as she looked him straight in the eyes and said, "Christianna of the house of Massah." She watched his eyes carefully. She could tell much by watching a person's eyes. They seemed to be the windows of a man's soul. What made them spark, she wondered, when I told him my name? Did he know that Massah meant contention? Oh, how fitly it described her life and the warfare of her soul.

"Christianna! Christianna, I am delighted. God has guided me in the way, for it is to visit you that I have come on this long journey."

His response so shocked and startled her that she suddenly felt faint. She put her hand to her head and looked quizzically into his face. Her knees felt as if they were going to buckle.

Sensing her unsteadiness, Eliezer motioned toward the nearby well. "Come, sit on the edge of the well for a moment."

Christianna felt foolish. What was wrong with her? How thankful she was for the edge of the well. "Excuse me, good sir, but I don't know what came over me," she said, taking a deep breath and gaining her composure. "Now, I pray thee, tell me why you, a servant of Shaddai, would come to see me. Why, I do not even know your master. And, as I told you, we are worlds apart. Why should God guide you to me? Pray tell, what would one such as you or your master have to do with me?" Christianna waited, again watching his eyes intently.

"Have you ever heard of my master's only son, Joshua?" Eliezer asked.

"Yes," Christianna responded wonderingly.

"What have you heard about him?"

"Only that he is like his father. Why?"

"Because," Eliezer said as he withdrew a parchment from the bag slung over his shoulder, "he has written you this."

Christianna stared at the parchment, incredulity written across her face.

"Take it . . . it's yours."

Why was her hand trembling? Had she not taught herself how to control her emotions—not to let others know what was going on inside? Yet here she was trembling inwardly and outwardly.

"Wha—what does it say?" she stammered. Why, she couldn't even talk without trembling!

"I do not know. I have not read it. It's for you from Joshua."

Consternation blanketed Christianna's face. "But why . . . why would Joshua, son of Shaddai, write to me? We have nothing in common. I told you before, we live in two different worlds."

"I know," Eliezer responded tenderly, "you do live in two different worlds. I don't know what is written in that scroll, but I do know why he wrote it."

By this time Christianna's head was bowed, slowly moving back and forth. Eliezer knew that her whole being was denying what she was hearing. He waited for her to lift her head and once again look him straight in the eyes. He knew she would as soon as she heard his words, "I do know why he wrote it."

Eliezer was right. He did not have to say, "Look at me." She was already looking and waiting.

The words came slowly, gently. "He loves you, Christianna."

Christianna's hand flew to her mouth, but not in time to stop the cry that came bursting forth from her lips. A flood of tears broke like a dam giving way, coursing down her face. Sobbing almost convulsively, she sprang to her feet, looked at him with brown, doe-like eyes wide with fright, and ran.

Before Eliezer could gain his composure, she was gone, leaving only the sound of her crying. They were not tears of joy.

CHAPTER
FOUR

C hristianna ran and ran, heading for the fields
where she could be alone. By now, because of her
intense sobbing, her chest felt as if it would
burst. It was hard enough to run, let alone run and cry at
the same time. Suddenly a sharp, knife-like pain caught
her side, and her hand dropped to the right side of her
abdomen as if to suppress the pain.

Slowing her pace, Christianna looked for
somewhere to hide. Spent and in pain, she dropped
down on a huge rock, threw her head back, eyes
opened wide, and cried in questioning agony,
"God . . . oh, God . . . what are You doing to me?
Tormenting me?" With that, she slid off the rock
and hit the ground with a hard thud. The parchment still in her hands, she wrapped her arms
around her knees and, burying her head between
her chest and knees, wept softly.

How long she wept she did not know. She only knew it was long enough for the sun to burn the back of her neck which had been left bare when her raven hair slipped over her shoulder. Finally, stiff and subdued, Christianna rose to her feet and began to walk, her head bowed, her feet kicking the numerous small stones that actually seemed to grow in Israel. "I thought I was hard like you, little stones, able to be walked on without budging, but now look! Someone has sent me tumbling." She looked again at the parchment scroll in her hand. It was wet with perspiration. Needing a respite from the heat of the sun, Christianna made her way to a small cave in the hillside.

The cave was comfortable, and its coolness seemed to revive her, enabling her to think more clearly. Christianna leaned back against the smooth rock and looked out over the valley below. After a few moments, she carefully untied the parchment and read:

> Joshua, son of Shaddai of Jerusalem, the great city of our God, to Christianna, daughter of Massah. Grace to you and peace in the name of the one true God.
>
> I know that it may seem very strange to you to receive a letter from me, one whom you have never seen and possibly have never even heard of

before Eliezer handed you the
parchment.

*Strange? You cannot know, Joshua, how strange it is!
Joshua! Oh, Joshua, suddenly you are more than a name
from another world. You are a person, real, made flesh and
bone. Yet who are you besides the son of Shaddai? Who are
you besides a young man of great wealth, spoken of with
reverence and awe? . . . Joshua.* Christianna liked
saying his name in her thoughts. *Joshua, are you
really as righteous, as holy, as good as they say you are?
And if so, Joshua, why would you write to me? Or how
could you ever . . .* The tears started to flow again, for
Christianna could not, even in her mind, say "love
me." She went back to the parchment.

> I am writing to you because I want
> you to come to know me. Someday,
> hopefully, you will love me as I,
> Christianna, love you. Oh, I can just
> hear you now, "Love me! How can he
> love me when he does not even know
> me?"

*Joshua . . . you are right. That is my question! But it
goes even deeper.* Christianna laid her head back
against her stone support and closed her eyes. Yet
even then the tears silently stole down her olive
cheeks. *Oh, Joshua, if you only knew, if you only really*

knew all about me, inside and out, you would never love me. You couldn't. If you are as they say you are . . . or if you even live as they say you live . . . there is no way you could ever love me. You are righteous. I am unrighteous. You are holy. I am unholy. You are good. Oh, Joshua, Joshua . . . I know my heart. It is wicked, deceitful . . . oh, so deceitful and so desperately wicked. No! No! Joshua, one such as you could never love one such as me. Yet if you are as I have heard you are, you would never use me for your pleasure and then cast me away when the sweetness of forbidden fruit became sour to you.

Christianna sat with her back to the wall, eyes closed, as the tears seeped down her cheeks. She couldn't stop them. They were tears that had been dammed up for years. Now Eliezer's words, "He loves you, Christianna," had cracked the stone walls of the dam. The shock of hearing that someone such as Joshua, son of Shaddai, could love her, whether it was true or not, had caused an earthquake in her soul that had cracked that impenetrable stone wall—a wall she had built herself, a wall meant to dam up all emotions that would make her vulnerable to a world she despised, yet must live in.

The sound of a vulture just outside the cave startled her out of her thoughts. Opening her eyes, she stared at the repulsive predator feasting on the carcass of some poor creature.

Even when you're dead, they feed on you, wanting only to fill their own bellies. Oh, Joshua, Joshua, are you a vulture like everyone else? Do you devour even the dead? I'm dead, Joshua. I'm dead. There is no life in me . . . not really. I'm only a survivor, a dog like Cur, only appreciated if I can entertain or bring others pleasure. Otherwise, I am kicked, unwanted, a vagabond, worth nothing to anyone. Love! What is love, Joshua? You say you love me. Do you know what love is? I don't. So if you love me, how can I love you back?

Christianna picked up the parchment. Her eyes drifted over the scroll until she found those familiar words. Strange . . . she didn't believe them. She couldn't comprehend them. But she wanted to read them again.

> I am writing to you because I want you to come to know me. Someday, hopefully, you will love me as I, Christianna, love you. Oh, I can just hear you now, "Love me! How can he love me when he does not even know me?" Oh, but, my beloved . . .

My beloved. Christianna savored the words for a minute, then she continued to read.

> . . . I do know you. I know all about you, and I love you just as you are. I know your father is a Jew, your mother a

Gentile. I know where you live. I know it's hard, and I know life has taken its toll on you. Yet you are a scrapper, a fighter, a survivor. I also know, Christianna, that you have encircled yourself with a high tower of stones to keep from being hurt. I know that your heart is hard and cold. But, oh, Christianna, turn to me, respond to my love, and I will give you a new heart, a heart that will cause you to love me always and not turn away from me.

How does he know? How does he know what's inside me? I've never shared it with anyone. Who would listen anyway? No, these are things he's guessing. He could not know what I have locked up inside.

Christianna read on. There had to be a flaw somewhere. On some point Joshua would be wrong. She had to find it. She had to, for then she could throw the parchment away. Then it wouldn't be true. Therefore, she could disregard it, forget she had ever read it, forget she had ever heard of Joshua!

But could she? Even . . . even if it were not true, could she forget this day, forget his words? Wasn't this something she had longed for all her life? She had so wanted to be loved unconditionally, whether she was Jew or Gentile, well or sick, pretty or ugly, rich or poor . . . loved just the way she was, even though he knew all about her. To be loved forever and ever, to belong, to never ever be forsaken or abandoned no matter what. She rolled the parchment to read on.

I realize all of this must come as quite a shock. You might even wonder why I have waited so long to declare my love to you. Suffice it to say, Christianna, that now is the right time. Before now, Beloved One, you could not have received it. Oh, I know it is difficult even now to comprehend, but in the days to come you shall see the wisdom of it all.

I have said enough for now. Just one last thing, and that will be sufficient for you this day. My father loves you also. He has chosen you for me, and I heartily concur. We are one in this decision. Now, Christianna, you have only to say yes . . . but not now. You will know when. First you must come to know me. For when you do turn to me, I want it to be with all your heart. Once you come to me, Christianna, you will be mine forever, and I, yours. Also when you come to me, I want you to know that I really do know all about you. This, my beloved, is not to intimidate you, but rather that you might know I love you unconditionally.

When the time is right, Eliezer will bring the kesubah for me. He will stand as my representative, and should you accept the covenant agreement, he will drink of the cup for me. At that time you will know the price I shall pay for you. During our betrothal period I shall be preparing a place for you in my father's house. When this is complete, I shall come for you.

Until then, Christianna, you shall not see me. Our betrothal, Beloved, shall be different than others. I have seen you, but you have never seen me. You never shall until I come for you. However, I want you to love me though you have never seen me. Believe in me, Christianna, and someday you will greatly rejoice with joy inexpressible and full of glory.

For now, Eliezer will bring you my letters one by one. Read them carefully, for they are written just for you. It is in these that I shall openly share all about myself. Also, my chosen one, I will tell you all about yourself so that you might understand why you are the way you are and so that you may know how you might become all that God created you to be.

There is one thing I will share—something you must know. You must know, you must understand, what it will mean to be mine . . . to be my bride, my wife, my co-laborer. I cannot take you to be my wife on your terms. It must be on my terms. Therefore, you must fully understand the cost of your commitment to me. Count the cost as you read my letters and know that our relationship must be preeminent, above all other relationships . . . even above your own desires or your own life.

That, Beloved, is one of the primary reasons for my letters to you. My decision is made. We, my father and I, have chosen you. Now the decision is yours. Do not let these next words upset you. Someday you will understand. Just know that I know your decision. When you do call to me, I will be waiting. Then, beloved Christianna, when you say, "Yes," you will begin to comprehend the breadth, the length, the height, the depth of my love for you . . . a love which surpasses all knowledge. Your life someday, Christianna, will be exceedingly abundantly beyond all you can ask or think. Why? Because, Christianna, I, Joshua, son of Shaddai, love you unconditionally and with all my being.

Christianna read Joshua's letter over and over again until the next one came. The cave became "theirs." There she would spread out all his letters and then talk to him in her heart, sharing her joys, her fears.

He did know her! He really did! Nowhere could she find him wrong. Sometimes when she read his letters, she laughed. But usually she read and wept. Now, however, they were not the tears of years of pent-up emotions. Some were tears of mourning over her sins and shortcomings. Others were tears of joy, inexplicable joy. From all she read, she knew more and more that Joshua truly did love her unconditionally. Never did he condemn her.

Her question now was, "Am I willing to love him preeminently?" With this, she struggled. For she knew he would not take her on lesser terms.

CHAPTER FIVE

*C*hristianna danced around the room, holding the veil to her face. *The music was of her own making as she sang, "I am my beloved's and he is mine . . . and his desire is toward me." Around and around she spun as over and over she said, "I am my beloved's. I am my beloved's," until finally she fell to the floor. Although she was giddy from twirling, she was careful not to let her veil touch the dirt floor of her family's home.*

Clutching the veil to her breast, she rocked back and forth. *Oh, Joshua, Joshua, you called me Beloved when there was nothing lovely about me. Just through your letters you have taught me to love simply by loving me. Oh, Joshua, how I wish I could see you! How I wish this were the day of our wedding rather than the day of our betrothal. How I wish . . .*

Christianna began to giggle. *I talk to him all the time as if he were visibly at my side.* Still giggling, she continued talking. *How I wish, my invisible husband,*

*that you could see me walk through the streets in my veil.
Now all will know I am betrothed. All the young men who
would have had me, but not in marriage, will now see that
there is one who wants me. Oh, Joshua, wait until . . .*
Christianna's hand flew to her mouth in a gesture of
surprise. Then with a giddy hilarity in her voice,
she said, *Wait until they find out it is you, Joshua. You!
Son of Shaddai of Jerusalem!*

No sooner had she spoken than her giggles were
abruptly covered by a cloud of concern that obliterated her joy. She was on her feet in a bound, both
hands on her hips. "They'll never believe me!
They'll never believe my father! They'll never
believe my mother. They'll think we are insane!
Addled! Under some demon's possession! Ohhh—
what will I do?" Christianna cried. "They'll laugh. I
can hear them now, 'Joshua, son of Shaddai, marry
you? You're crazy! Why would he marry you when
he could have any virgin daughter of Israel?
Besides, such a son of Israel would never become
one with a Gentile-Jew!'"

That was what the Jews called her. Always,
because of her Gentile blood, there was a high wall
between them . . . the Law, the Covenants, the
Pentateuch. None of these belonged to her, they
said, because she was a half-breed. No, they would
never believe her. Now the joy of the veil was
dampened by the anticipated unbelief of the people.

"Christianna, Christianna!" Her father's voice
was unusually high, even squeaky, "He's coming!

Eliezer is coming! I saw him from the roof. Hurry! Prepare yourself. We cannot keep one as distinguished as he waiting." By the time her father finished calling, Christianna was standing behind him listening to him mutter, "My, oh, my."

"My, oh, my! Father, what are you my-oh-mying about?" Christianna tenderly questioned her father. Such a love for him now flooded her heart. Oh, how could she have hated him so? Was it he or she who had changed? Silly question. Joshua's love shed abroad in her heart now flowed out freely to others, even to Christianna's amazement. And it had not gone unnoticed. According to the gossip her mother heard from the women at the well and in the market, all their village was talking about the change they had seen come over Christianna.

Maybe, Christianna thought, *maybe they will believe me since they have seen a change in me. Maybe they'll realize, since I don't lie anymore or act snappy, that I'm not lying now.* The possibility brought joy back into the occasion. Turning her thoughts back to her father, she again asked, "Father dear, what are you my-oh-mying about?"

"About the bridal price, my dear, the bridal price! They are a wealthy family you know, the wealthiest, finest family in all Israel. I still . . . I still can't understand it. Maybe people of their position can get away with anything."

"Understand? Get away with? Father, what on earth are you talking about?"

"Now, Christianna, don't be upset, but I just cannot understand why such a father and son would choose you, my daughter. We are not rich, nor wise, nor mighty, nor noble. Rather, the house of Massah is weak, base, and despised. Why? Why would they choose you . . . us?" Massah was flustered. He did not want to hurt Christianna. In his own way he loved her, but he just couldn't figure it out. Why Joshua? Oh, well! Maybe God was finally smiling on him in good fortune.

"Well, Father dear, one thing we are not able to do is boast. We have nothing to boast about. I never could begin to earn or deserve whatever Joshua is willing to pay for me."

"Massah, Massah! He's here!"

Everyone's voice is of a higher pitch today, even Momma's, thought Christianna.

"Hurry, Massah! Come to the door. I cannot greet him alone. Massah!" Bernice called again.

"Wife, I'm here. Calm yourself. You sound like a bellowing camel!"

Then, turning to the approaching figure, he said, "Eliezer, may the peace of God be upon you as you enter our humble dwelling."

Massah's voice was no longer trembling. He had risen beautifully to the occasion. Of course, he had been practicing his greeting for days, rehearsing with his wife and daughter where each would stand

and what each would do. This was one occasion in which Massah had thought he never would participate. He really had not expected anyone to take Christianna for a wife. Oh, she was lovely enough, but her behavior. Her personality. Who could ever tolerate such a woman day and night? Yet miraculously she was changing right before his eyes. Still there was more that could stand improving. Maybe someday a man could tolerate her. A smile broke over his face as he thought, *Oh, well, after today, if she says yes—and she assured me she would—then she is no longer my burden. She belongs to Joshua. I must only keep her a virgin until her wedding day.* Massah almost sighed with relief.

"Massah, I have come as a friend of the bridegroom, Joshua, son of Shaddai, to present to you a marriage covenant," said Eliezer.

"Eliezer, I greet you in the stead of Joshua and Shaddai. How I do wish they could have honored us with their presence. However, Christianna has explained to me the desires of Joshua and Shaddai in all this matter, and I humbly submit. My brother, Shemiah, shall act as my deputy. But first may I have the honor of serving you some refreshment?"

Eliezer, honoring the custom of betrothal, responded even as had his namesake when he set out for Abraham to procure a bride for Isaac. "I will not eat until I have told of my business."

Christianna smiled. She was enjoying every moment of this ritual. Never, never had she ever dreamed that such a moment would be hers. One so fine, so proper, so honorable! Only one thing kept it from being all she wanted—if only Joshua and Shaddai were here. Besides, if they were here, then all the village would know that it was really Joshua, the Joshua of the house of Shaddai! With that thought her shoulders squared and her chest rose in triumph. But she diminished quickly to her normal posture as once again she wondered if they would ever believe her. Oh, well, she would not let it spoil her joy. She was still a scrapper. Whether they believed it or not, she felt that somehow she would find a way to convince them. *Oh, how I wish I could see him! Is he handsome? Strong? Tall enough? Oh, I pray he is just right.* These thoughts plagued her a lot lately, for never in all his letters had Joshua told Christianna what he looked like.

Quickly she was brought back to the occasion at hand as Shemiah stepped forward to ask the bride's price. Her part of accepting or refusing the contract came next. But first came the dowry. They must see if the dowry was suitable. The price normally was high enough to make it a sacrifice on the part of the bridegroom, but suppose Joshua tried to skimp because of who she was or because she had already told him she would be his wife. Christianna's hand flew to her mouth to hide her lips as she whispered a secret prayer to Jehovah. "Oh, Jehovah, Adonai . . . don't let him skimp. Don't let him make my dowry less than if I were a queen and he a king."

While Christianna was praying, Massah was hopping from one foot to the other like a little boy who couldn't wait to see what was hidden behind his rich uncle's back. Never before had a man who represented such wealth even come to the door of his humble dwelling. What kind of price had Shaddai authorized Eliezer to pay? Massah could barely contain himself.

Christianna's mother, Bernice, just waited. She didn't anticipate much. When Christianna had first shared part of Joshua's letter professing his love, her mother was quick with advice—advice born of bitterness, "The only good thing about marrying Joshua is the fact that he is rich and, being rich, he can buy your acceptance. Remember, it's not going to be easy when people find out you have the blood of Gentile dogs in you!" Bernice spoke with bitter sarcasm. She had been wounded too often by the rapier-like edge of gossiping tongues. Too often had she rehearsed the mistakes of her past, of her marriage to Massah.

Now Bernice thought again of the warning she had given her daughter in days past. "If you listen to me, you will dangle the bait before Joshua and keep him waiting for your 'yes' until you hear the price he will pay for you. One thing I can guarantee, my stubborn daughter. Once he knows that you are his, your dowry will be as low as it can be. Watch and see! Mark my words!" Bernice's voice was sharp and her words clipped. "Then, what will you have should he ever divorce you?"

"But, Mother, Joshua said he would never—" Christianna was interrupted almost as soon as she started.

"Christianna, all a Jewish woman has is her dowry, the fine clothes, and jewels she takes into her marriage. And you have no headgear with coins, no jewelry. Why, if Joshua does not pay much for you, you will be a pauper living in the midst of wealth but without any security." With that Bernice had looked straight at her daughter and said, "As your father promised, all you will have is half of the dowry Joshua pays for you. Half for you, half for your father. Your father will not go back on his word. The fool thinks it is going to be a good dowry." Bernice spoke slowly and purposefully at this point. "Also, he expected to have you on his hands all his life. That is why he has been so generous."

As Bernice recalled her advice to her daughter, she felt a twinge of guilt. To justify her words she thought, *I sounded harsh, I know, but someone has to set Christianna straight. Being in love with Joshua has made her giddy enough about life. What will happen to her if she doesn't face reality? She must be prepared for the worst, for this marriage couldn't be as good as it sounds. Somewhere there has to be a catch. I can't figure it out. Probably, as I told her, the dowry will be nothing, or perhaps Joshua is deformed or something, or maybe he has spells no one knows about.*

Bernice reeled, almost losing her balance, as her personal reverie was broken by what she had just vaguely heard. Before she could stop herself, the words were out of her mouth, interrupting Eliezer right in the middle of his speech. Almost gasping she said, "What did you say?"

Bernice's question and impropriety shocked all who were in the room. Yet Massah and Shemiah were secretly pleased that she had asked Eliezer to repeat his words, for they could not believe their ears either!

Christianna, once again watching Eliezer's eyes, caught the twinkle as he repeated himself. "The dowry or bride's price shall be to the house of Massah and Bernice a new dwelling, consisting of two stories, built around a large court. The house will be constructed of the best stone available and tiled with the finest mosaics."

Christianna's mother was so thrilled she did not mind eating her words. Who would ever have dreamed she should be the mistress of such a home?

Eliezer continued, "The house shall be built on a fine piece of ground already purchased for this very purpose. The land is of adequate size to pasture my master's gift of one hundred sheep and one hundred bullocks to the house of Massah."

Now it was Massah's turn. His anxious dancing had stopped. Suddenly he became as rigid as stone, his feet glued to the floor. Overwhelmed, he could not move. Or was he afraid to move for fear he would wake up?

"Also—"

Also! Massah thought. *Also! I don't know if I can stand an "also." My heart is about to beat out of my robe now!*

Eliezer proceeded, eyes still twinkling. He wouldn't have missed this for anything. "Also, there shall be paid to Massah and to Bernice one hundred silver coins each and one hundred gold coins each. Now, for Christianna. First, she shall receive unlimited funds, not to be abused, but to be used to provide her every need until the day of the consummation of the covenant agreement of marriage."

Now it was Christianna's turn to be shocked. Just as her mother had, Christianna stammered, "Wh—what?"

"Christianna," Eliezer said, looking her square in the eyes, "my master shall supply all your needs in accordance with all his wealth. Then, on the day of the consummation of this covenant, you, Christianna, shall enter into a joint inheritance with Joshua of all that belongs to Shaddai."

At these words, Christianna fainted. Who had ever heard of such a thing happening to a woman in Israel, let alone happening to a half-breed! Bernice screamed and Massah slumped onto the nearest stool. Shemiah was about to die. He wanted to be the first to tell everyone in the village about the marriage contract he had negotiated! By now all propriety was forgotten as Bernice grabbed the covenant cup and forced some of the rich red wine between Christianna's lips in an attempt to revive her daughter.

When Christianna had been revived and most of the confusion had subsided, Eliezer spoke again. This time, however, his voice became very solemn, bringing a deadening silence to all.

"Finally, Christianna, Joshua wants you to know that should you agree to this covenant of marriage, nothing you would ever do could cause him to break this covenant. Joshua's covenant of marriage is an unconditional, everlasting covenant. From this day forward, if you agree to this covenant, he will put into writing that he will never divorce you under any circumstance. Cloths of virginity from your wedding night need not be saved or used by your parents. You are betrothed forever, to become one in flesh when Joshua comes to take you to his father's house. Now then, when Shaddai approves Joshua's preparations for you, he shall send Joshua to bring you to their home. Until then you must be patient, for Joshua knows not the day nor the hour when his father shall permit him to come for you.

"In turn, Christianna," Eliezer continued, "Joshua asks only one thing of you, and that is that you would love him with all your heart, with all your soul, with all your mind, and with all your strength."

At that, Bernice whispered in Christianna's ear, "Forgive me, my daughter. The well of my heart has brought forth only bitter water. I did not know. I did not dream—"

Shemiah's call to Christianna halted Bernice's words. "Christianna, as deputy of the house of Massah I must ask you, do you agree to this marriage covenant?" After all he had heard, Shemiah, deputy or not, felt almost foolish asking Christianna that question.

For herself, Christianna had heard enough. Jehovah had answered her prayer exceedingly abundantly, just as Joshua had promised to love her . . . exceedingly abundantly above all she could ask or think. "I do, Shemiah," she said. "I agree to accept this dowry on behalf of my father, Massah, my mother, Bernice, and myself, and I do plight Joshua, son of Shaddai, my troth."

Shemiah continued, "Eliezer, as you stand in Joshua's stead, will you drink of the cup of the covenant, thereby sealing this agreement before God?"

Eliezer responded by stepping forward to receive the cup from Christianna's hand. Having drunk of the cup, he said, "I, Joshua, do drink thee, Christianna, bone of my bone, flesh of my flesh."

Eliezer then pressed the cup to Christianna's lips. Having drunk of the cup, she said, "I, Christianna, do drink thee, Joshua, bone of my bone, flesh of my flesh."

As she finished, Eliezer leaned closer to her and whispered, "My master loves you, Christianna, more than himself. Be true to him. Love him whom you have not yet seen. Don't ever forget that the spirit is willing but the flesh is weak! Walk circumspectly, my daughter. Do not abuse his unconditional love."

Abuse such love . . . how could I? What a strange thing to say to me. Oh, I wish Eliezer had not said that. Why, I never could be unfaithful now . . . or could I? Christianna trembled at the thought, as if touched by a sudden chill. *Oh, Joshua, come for me soon . . . come quickly!*

CHAPTER
SIX

After the betrothal Christianna's days were filled with preparation. There was material to be procured, the finest of white linen. Christianna would make her own gown and prepare her own ornaments. Now that Joshua had agreed to supply all her needs, there was no necessity to borrow another's garments or jewels. Her jewels and her robe would be her own to treasure forever. All must be perfect in every way. Christianna's heart's desire was to be beautifully adorned for her husband. Thus every stitch was carefully measured, every seam exquisitely bound. Inside and out, her wedding robe must be perfect.

Christianna knew that, according to custom, she probably had at least a year between her betrothal and the actual wedding. Well, it would take her a year. But maybe if she hurried, Joshua would hurry. Maybe the time would pass quickly.

Oh, there was so much to do! Bridesmaids must be chosen. Chains of pearls and gold beads must be strung and woven for her hair. Her body must be oiled with the finest of oils until her skin had a luster of golden marble. Flowers and spices must be gathered for perfumes. It was all so exciting . . . and sometimes overwhelming. For on top of everything, she and her parents were eagerly overseeing the construction of their new home. There was not much for them to do, for Joshua had hired the most skilled of laborers. Yet it was hard to stay away. Never had they dreamed of such a home. Besides, it was fun to share it with their friends . . . what friends they had, that is!

Some who had professed to be friends became jealous over Massah's good fortune. Others, as Christianna had imagined, simply refused to believe that a betrothal had taken place. How they explained Massah's sudden good fortune apart from a dowry was another thing. When men do not want to believe the truth, willful ignorance conjures up all sorts of rationalizations, excuses, or denials.

"They're crazy," some of the townspeople said. "There's no Shaddai, no Joshua. Who has ever seen them?"

"Just rumors, that's all."

"Myths that do not exist."

"Figments of their imagination."

Others, who could not deny their existence, denied such a betrothal. "If Shaddai and Joshua are all we've heard they are, would they choose the likes of Christianna? Would they not choose some fine virgin of wealth and position? The daughter of a Pharisee or a Sadducee? Or even the virgin daughter of one of the Sanhedrin? They are the rulers of Israel. Wealth and position always intermarry."

Still others hurled ugly accusations. "You're possessed by Beelzebub!"

Most, however, left it with, "You said he's coming. We'll believe it when we see it."

The year passed quickly for Christianna—and what a year it was. Never had she felt more like a woman. Gone were the days when she had agreed with the Pharisees that one of the worst things a human being could be was a woman. Many were the times when she had heard them on the street corners praying long prayers, sometimes saying, "O God, I thank Thee that Thou hast not made me a dog, a Gentile, or a woman!"

However, Christianna also had known her share of rejection that year, for when her father had extended Shaddai's invitation to the wedding feast, many had refused the offer. Some had said that they were sure they would still be working in the new fields they had purchased and would not be able to attend. Others had begged off, saying that they must devote their time to their new wives. All seemed too busy, too occupied with themselves and their own selfish world.

On one of his many visits, Eliezer had brought wedding garments for all those who had been invited to the marriage supper, for custom held that no one, absolutely no one, was permitted to attend the feast without a wedding garment. Yet relatively few would take a garment, even though they were freely given. Somehow most of those invited just couldn't believe that Joshua and Shaddai had chosen such a one as Christianna.

As the first year of her betrothal came to an end, Christianna's longing for Joshua increased. Surely any night now she would hear trumpets in the street and would finally behold her beloved Joshua for the first time. Night after night she dreamed of his coming. Yet some of her dreams bordered on nightmares, for sometimes she found herself unprepared. Her gown was nowhere to be found! Frantically she and her mother would search their new home, looking in every nook and cranny, only to find her bridal dress soiled or unfinished.

Dreams like these caused Christianna to awaken, drenched in perspiration. Many times after such a night she would climb to the roof of their home where she would sit and think of Joshua's words . . . words that admonished her to be watching and waiting for his coming.

Christianna had memorized some of his letters from beginning to end. It was on nights like these, when she felt so alone, that she would rehearse them over and over again.

> Christianna, I will come, in all probability, on a day, in an hour, in which you think not. Oh, Beloved, even I do not know when. Only my father knows. But when all things are ready and Father gives me leave, I shall come quickly. I know that it is hard to wait, to be constantly prepared, to anticipate and then not have it come to pass as you have planned or desired. But be assured, **I shall come.**

Those last three words had been written in bold characters. Remembering them, Christianna smiled.

> Keep yourself pure, keep your garments clean. Be on the alert, for you know not the day or the hour when I, your Lord, your loving Lord, shall

come. I so desire, my beloved, to
receive you to myself as a chaste virgin.

Joshua's letters had been less frequent in recent
months. However, Christianna had dutifully read
and reread all those she had received. Joshua had
admonished her to do so.

Since, my beloved, they shall keep
you ever mindful of the high position to
which you are called.

Joshua had explained that his letters were like a
textbook that would school her for life. How right
he was! As she read them, she learned great truths
about how her life with Joshua was to be lived. Yet
his letters were not simply filled with teaching.
Sometimes when she read them, she felt rebuked!
How often his words exposed something evil in her
heart or her deeds. Sometimes her shame was so
great that she mourned deeply, wondering how
Joshua could love one so poor and so destitute of
anything worth commendation.

Yet always when his words wounded, they also
healed. They always gave her a ray of hope as they
carefully explained how to correct that which was so
desperately wrong. What wisdom Joshua had! For it
was here in his letters that Christianna learned how
to live a righteous life. Why, she was actually being

transformed through reading Joshua's letters. And others saw it besides Christianna. More and more, his words exposed the frivolity of the world, its wisdom and its ways. It was as if a veil had been taken off her eyes. What she saw dimly before, she now saw clearly.

It was to all these words she clung, claiming Joshua's promises, believing that at any time he might come. Without them, she knew she could not survive the waiting!

Periodically, Christianna would visit those who had agreed to be her bridesmaids. During each visit she would remind them to make sure their lamps were filled with oil. "You know," she would say laughingly, "how the groom usually comes at night. You'd better be ready to go when you hear that trumpet sound!"

Sometimes one of them would teasingly reply, "Are you sure he'll come? Maybe he'll change his mind!"

To which Christianna would confidently respond, "And should a man sacrifice so much to buy a bride and not come to take her to wife? He has decked me with ornaments, put bracelets upon my hands, a chain upon my neck, a jewel upon my forehead, earrings in my ears, and a beautiful crown upon my head. He shall come to claim his own!"

But when? The days of waiting turned into weeks, the weeks into months, and the months into another year. Why? Why hadn't Joshua come? As far as Christianna was concerned, there was nothing to hold him back.

As the months of waiting grew unbearably long, Christianna read Joshua's letters less and less. Oh, usually she found something new each time she did read them, but they began to bore her. Duty held her attention only for a time. It seemed as if her first joy of love and ardor was seeping away. Time and time again she would walk through the marketplace, over the fields, to their cave, where she would pour out her heart to a man who was not there.

Oh, if only I knew what you looked like, Joshua, if only you were here in flesh and blood for me to see, to talk to . . . to touch. Why, oh, why couldn't our betrothal have been like others. I need the reality of you. You, Joshua. Not Eliezer! Not your letters! I'm lonely, so lonely. And I'm human, Joshua, I'm human . . . made of flesh. Oh, why don't you come? Why don't you take me? I need you.

In his letters, Joshua had warned her about times like these.

Set your affections on the things
that belong to us, not on the things of
this world. Let my words dwell in you

richly. They will take you through the dark and lonely times. Don't lose heart. Beware of the world and its lusts. Remember, its pleasures only last for a season. Watch yourself lest you be tempted.

But Christianna didn't heed his words.

CHAPTER SEVEN

*C*hristianna was in a frightful mood! Why, oh, why had she listened to those girls at the well? She knew better. She had listened to sensual female tales like that before . . . before Joshua had come into her life. It had frustrated her then; it frustrated her now. Never had she been more aware of being a woman, longing to be held . . . to be touched . . . to experience the mysteries, the anticipation, the thrill of romance.

"O God, I must not think this way." As Christianna muttered aloud, a hint of bitterness mixed with self-pity crept into her voice. "I am betrothed. Married, but not taken. How much can I take? How long can I wait?"

Christianna put on her veil out of duty, not pride. No betrothed woman went anywhere without her veil. Whenever she stepped out of the house, all must know that she had already been claimed in marriage, for to be betrothed in Israel meant to be married.

Once outside, Christianna looked at the *mezuza* that had been put on the doorpost, as Joshua had instructed. She dutifully brushed it with her hand and then went on her way. *I need to walk, to be spent, to be so exhausted that when it comes time to sleep I can fall into bed and be done with this longing!* Joshua was nowhere in her thoughts. It had been several weeks since she had read his letters. Oh, the wedding garment, ornaments, and jewels were all laid out in her room, still waiting for the sound of the trumpet heralding Joshua's coming! But her robe had grown dusty, and Christianna had grown weary of looking at it. Its newness and beauty had worn off. She had even grown tired of trying it on. The zeal of her first love had waned with the passing of time and with the humdrum affairs of day-to-day living.

In no time Christianna found herself in the marketplace. The vigor of her walk in the heat of the day had created a thirst. Reaching into her waist-band, Christianna extracted some coins to see if she had enough to stop at one of the stands and get something to drink. As she stood there preoccupied with counting them, she suddenly jumped with fright, sending her coins rolling through the dust on the ground.

"Cur! Cur, what are you doing, you bad dog, frightening me that way? Now see what you made me do! How will I ever find those brass coins in all this dirt?'' Christianna was exasperated.

Although she talked to Cur, her voice carried a tone he wasn't used to; nor was she giving him her usual friendly attention. He wanted petting or a morsel of food, not just a scolding. So as Christianna squatted in the marketplace, running her fingers through the dirt as she gathered up her coins, Cur began barking at her. Christianna, too preoccupied to be bothered, continued her searching. So Cur ran straight at her, caught her sleeve in his mouth, and began his tug-of-war, growling loudly. Christianna's veil hid her smile as she quickly gave her sleeve a jerk, sending him flying. Now the game was on! He had her attention! Delighted, Cur began to bark, darting at her repeatedly, attempting once again to lay hold of her sleeve.

Amused, yet still busy looking for her coins, Christianna at first did not know what caused Cur to suddenly yelp so. It was a yelp followed by a pitiful whine.

"Cur, Cur . . . what's wr—" Suddenly a rock came hurling through the air headed straight for the dog. Deftly Christianna tried to stop its flight with her hand. "Oh—oh—oh, that hurts." Wincing with pain and filled with anger, she forgot who she was and where she was. "You . . . you . . ." she couldn't think for a moment what to call him. "You fool! What are you doing? Leave that poor dog alone.

Throw stones at someone who can throw stones back, you coward."

"I beg your pardon." The voice sounded half amused, half indignant. "I was only trying to rescue you from an attacking dog. And is this what I get for coming to your rescue—to be called a fool rather than a protector? Why, that dog had you practically on the ground. Look at you. You're covered with dust."

Christianna looked down at her dusty robe, then raised her head to look at the young man standing before her. As she did, her eyes caught his. In all the commotion with Cur her veil had fallen to the side of her head, and the man was staring at her, pleasure written across his countenance. For a moment their eyes locked. Then in an almost defiant boldness, in one glance, his eyes caressed her body! Her eyes never left his, and she saw the way he looked at her. Suddenly her whole body felt like it was on fire, and her face was hot, as if burnished by too much sun.

Holding her injured right hand with her left, she began gesturing toward the ground. "I . . . I dropped my coins. You see I was thirsty . . . I had walked so fast . . . Cur, the dog, wanted to play . . . I usually bring him food." *I'm not making sense*, Christianna thought, as she tried to explain herself. *What's wrong with me?*

"Tarry a minute." He laughed as he spoke. "You're talking in a foreign tongue. I cannot keep up with you. Calm yourself."

Christianna was not talking in a foreign tongue, but she knew what this young man meant. She also knew that what she was feeling was not good. She should walk away immediately, but everything within her wanted to stay. Mustering all the composure she could, she said, "Excuse me. My hand is hurting, and I'm not thinking—"

The next thing Christianna knew a thousand thrills went coursing through her veins, for he had reached out, taken her hand in his, and ever so gently begun to rub away the dirt from around the abrasion on the palm of her hand.

Quickly, Christianna jerked her hand from his. "Thank you, but I'm fine. Shalom." He didn't look Jewish, but she did not know what else to say. Abruptly she turned toward home.

"Please, please don't leave. I want to talk with you. Allow me to introduce myself. I'm Kosmos." His voice became louder as he tried to keep pace with Christianna, who by now was almost running.

Suddenly Christianna had become aware of her surroundings and of the fact that she, a betrothed woman, was standing unveiled in the middle of the marketplace talking to a stranger—a man. Guilt overwhelmed her, though not because of what had happened but because of how she felt inside. She wanted to talk to this . . . what was his name? Kosmos? She had never heard a name like that.

Christianna turned, reaching for her dangling veil and covering her face at the same time. "I am a betrothed woman of Israel," she said, "and it is not fitting that I should be talking to you, a stranger. I pray thee excuse me." However, even as she prepared to leave, she searched his eyes. Once more she wanted to feel what she had felt before. She was not disappointed. Kosmos smiled and looked at her with unabashed appreciation.

Christianna had difficulty sleeping that night. For a while she sat by her oil lamp and tried to read Joshua's last letter, but her mind kept drifting back to the marketplace. Over and over she rehearsed what had happened. Each time she tried to remember more about him. His face. His build. The coarse strength of his hand. The softness of his touch. *Was Joshua as handsome as this young man? Where is he from? Why have I not seen him before? To what country does he belong? Will I ever see him again?*

Such questions filled her thoughts. Questions about Kosmos, not Joshua. There was a mystery about him, an element of the unknown that was exciting. *Seductive! That's what Kosmos is . . . seductive!* Desire flooded her being.

Lying upon her bed, Christianna let her imagination run unchecked. She had forgotten Joshua's words admonishing her to bring every thought captive . . . to think only on things that were lovely, true, and virtuous.

Finally sleep came, and with it, dreams. This time Joshua had a face. Or was it Joshua?

CHAPTER EIGHT

Christianna braided and rebraided her hair the next morning, giving it meticulous attention. As she carefully selected her robe, she hummed a new ballad she had heard one of her friends singing. Slipping on her sandals, she walked onto the balcony overlooking the center courtyard. Joshua had made all this possible—a selection of robes, a beautiful home, a courtyard—but she had begun to take it for granted. As Christianna had grown accustomed to her new style of life, her once heartfelt gratitude and sense of awe at the bestowal of such blessings had diminished. Sometimes she even felt she deserved it all. Why, after all, shouldn't she have it?

"Where are you going?" she called down, seeing her mother crossing the courtyard.

"To the market. Today's the day they expect the fruit to come in and—"

"Wait, Mother. I'll go for you."

"Well, that's a surprise! But if you want to, it would certainly be a blessing to me. Your father wants me to prepare him a fresh kid today, and I must bring one from the flocks."

As Christianna hurried out through the door behind her mother, her hand flew up to the *mezuza* out of habit. Yet this time the words from the Law of Moses, written on the parchment encased within this amulet, came to her mind: "Love the LORD . . . keep these words I am commanding you . . . teach them, talk of them . . . bind them as a sign on your forehead . . . to the doorposts of your house." Christianna had heard her father quote these words from the Law often. Today, however, other words also haunted her. Words that were not inside the *mezuza*, but which followed those words in the Law: "Watch thyself lest you forget the LORD. . . ."

Christianna stopped abruptly. *Maybe I shouldn't go,* she thought. *What will I do if I see him? Oh, that's silly! I'm sure he's gone.* But she wasn't sure. *Besides, I have to go to help Mother,* Christianna lied to herself. She wanted to see Kosmos. She wanted to find out if he was still in the village. She wanted to talk with him, to feel his eyes, his touch. Deep in her heart she knew her desire was wrong, but she still wanted it. Nothing else, nothing more, just that seemingly innocent thrill of flirting one more time . . . that pleasure that comes from a new and unexpected source . . . the inexplicably mysterious ecstasy of the moment.

Christianna roamed the marketplace for over an hour, stopping at every stall, conversing gaily with each merchant, wondering if perchance Kosmos might be watching her from a distance. She was full of gaiety . . . a gaiety that had been absent for a long time. Yet there was a nervousness about her. She searched each face. *Cur! If only I could find Cur. I could make him bark again and maybe. . . .* But Christianna could not find Cur.

Disappointed and feeling almost cheated, her effervescence gone, Christianna had started toward home when suddenly she stopped, looked at the sun, and thought, *Mother won't need me yet. Besides, I can't stand to go home.* She would walk through the fields . . . but not to the cave. She refused to think of Joshua today.

Just as she was leaving the marketplace, she saw him. She had turned back for one final look, and there he was . . . standing in the middle of the square looking all about him. When their eyes met, a smile, a warm ear-to-ear grin, broke out on his face. Christianna knew it was because of her. Dropping her head and eyes ever so slightly, she turned away and walked rapidly toward the fields. If he did follow, they would not be seen talking together. People just wouldn't understand.

Christianna never looked back again. She just walked, kicking an occasional stone, sending it joyfully skipping. Finally, she heard his voice behind her. "Whoa! Whoa! We're alone. We can talk now!"

Smart, isn't he? And it sounds like he knows it! Christianna stopped, turned around, and looked directly at him with her big, brown, doe-like eyes. "I am not a donkey. You needn't say 'Whoa.' My name is Christianna." Kosmos threw back his head and laughed, and it pierced her heart like an arrow. She loved it.

How wonderful it was to be in the presence of a man whose eyes held nothing but admiration for her as a woman. She reveled in her femininity! What fun it was to discover another, to watch his countenance, to enjoy the way he walked, to admire his maleness. Christianna was so tired of the company of women!

They had walked and talked for a long time before Christianna finally, cautiously, explained her situation to Kosmos—that she was betrothed to a very fine man whom she had never seen.

"You see, Kosmos, to a Jew, to be betrothed is for all intents and purposes to be married," Christianna explained, certain that Kosmos, being a Gentile, knew nothing of their customs. "It is a covenant which can only be broken by divorce, and then only for infidelity. But, of course, Joshua would never divorce me even for that," Christianna's voice was suddenly filled with pride, "for he loves me unconditionally. That's unusual, you know. Moses wrote in Deuteronomy—that's one of our books of the Law—that if a man takes a wife and does not find her a virgin, and she has no cloth that is evidence of her virginity, then she can be stoned. Of course, today they hardly ever stone women, but some are divorced."

Christianna seemed to stand a little taller as she looked with pride into Kosmos' face and said, "Yet Joshua said that even if I slipped, he would never put me away. He assured me that because we have pledged ourselves together in covenant, he would never leave me nor forsake me. Why, it's written right into our marriage agreement."

At that, Kosmos reached over and touched her chin with his fingers so that she could not turn away. Then he looked her straight in the eyes and said, "Christianna, if you were mine I would never allow another to touch you. You would either be mine alone or not at all."

The touch, the look, the words were so dramatic. For a moment, only a moment, Christianna wondered if Joshua really loved her. How could he love her with a passion and still accept her unconditionally or share her even once with another? Here was a relationship that was real—not one that was yet to be in some unknown, unseen, distant future. A relationship that . . . well, it was hard to explain. All Christianna knew was that she did not want it to end. She wanted Joshua, but she also wanted Kosmos.

Kosmos listened intently as Christianna told him that they could never be more than friends. "I'm betrothed. Joshua could come at any moment."

"How long have you been waiting, Christianna?"

"A bit over two years now," she replied with a hint of embarrassment in her voice.

"Two years! Two years!" Kosmos practically yelled it. "How could a man wait two years to take a woman like you to be his wife? Has he ever seen you?"

"Yes, but—" Christianna stammered.

"I would never make you wait. I could never wait. I wouldn't rest until you were mine, until I had devoured you, consumed you."

His words both pleased and disturbed. A seductive excitement warmed her; yet at the same time she was filled with a guilt which obliterated peace and joy. It was the same feeling she had experienced when they met in the marketplace. Her face was flushed. She had to walk.

Suddenly Kosmos was in front of her. Gesturing adamantly, arms extended, palms out, fingers spread wide, his face almost red with anger, he exclaimed, "Are you sure Joshua said those things to you? And if he said them, do you think he really meant them?" Kosmos' voice was getting louder, his hands giving emphasis to every sentence. "He's holding out on you, Christianna. He doesn't really love you. If he did, he would not make you wait. I know, I know. You say he's coming, but where is he?"

Suddenly, with great drama, he tossed his head back until he faced the sky above. Then he stood there shaking his head back and forth, saying, "How can he do this to you? How can he do this to you?" He turned and looked at her again. "You're young! You're beautiful! You have needs—desires that must be met. Christianna, dear, dear, Christianna, listen to me, believe me. Joshua does not love you. He could not love you and do this to you. He's lying to you."

Kosmos reached for her hand, but she drew it back. Suddenly she felt confused. She had to get away. *Oh, why did our day have to end this way?* She began slowly backing away from him as she talked. "Kosmos, I must go home. I must leave now. Mother is expecting me. Please don't follow me. No one would understand. Father would be furious. I must go." With that she turned and, half running, took off across the field.

Kosmos ran after her. "Wait! Wait! Can we talk again tomorrow? We could meet here in the field or in one of those caves? No one would know."

"I don't know, Kosmos. I'm confused. I can't think right now. Maybe in the fourth hour of the day . . . oh, I don't know . . . maybe not."

Kosmos seemed to choose his words carefully. "Christianna, I'll be here waiting. Should you come, you will not be kept waiting by me." She caught the inflection of his voice as he emphasized "by me."

Christianna could barely eat the delicious kid her mother had prepared, and she thought the evening meal would never end. All she wanted was to be alone, to think things through.

It was another long night . . . a night of tossing and turning as Christianna's thoughts churned. *Has Joshua been lying to me? Would love, real love, keep me waiting? Does he not desire me enough to hurry?* Suddenly fear gripped her heart. Suppose Joshua and Eliezer had lied. Suppose they had deceived her. Suppose Shaddai was dead and Joshua was really some wealthy, decrepit old man. Or suppose he had no home to take her to. Suppose all of this talk of supplying all her needs was only a ruse of some sort. Suppose he would keep her waiting until no man would want her.

What was it Kosmos said? Christianna tried to remember his every word; yet when she did, the words from Joshua's letters would come to her mind. She pushed them aside.

Finally, she slept . . . fitfully dreaming one nightmare after another.

CHAPTER NINE

C hristianna saw Kosmos the next day. She arrived at the field about the fifth hour. He was waiting. What a wonderful time they had simply laughing and talking. Oh, how Christianna enjoyed it! Joshua's name did not come up once in the course of conversation. Kosmos did not touch her, nor try to touch her. She was glad. That night there was no guilt over her emotions, for none had been aroused. She did not feel dirty, unclean, tainted. Rather, as she mused over their time together, Christianna began looking at herself in a new way.

Kosmos had reawakened her spark of independence. Plus he had caused her to see potential in herself that she had never seen before. What did she want? Think it, and it would be hers. That was what Kosmos had said.

"Christianna, you can do anything you set your

mind to! I've never seen a woman as capable as you. You're a scrapper, Christianna. And you're not a Jew. You're a Gentile too. Oh, Christianna, in the world where I come from, women are not slaves, chattels. Many have their own businesses. They travel. They are free, Christianna, free as God meant women to be. Surely your Jehovah did not create woman to be trampled underfoot by men. He meant for you to be happy, fulfilled, realizing your full potential!''

For several weeks now Kosmos and Christianna had been meeting in the field. She felt better about their relationship; she was not ashamed, for really there was nothing to be ashamed of—all her silly emotions were under control. Even though sometimes her desires would flare because of a look or an accidental touch, she had learned to deal with them right away.

After all, I am a woman, she reasoned, *I'm bound to feel this way. It's natural. I can control it. No need to flee and spoil a perfectly good friendship.*

Every evening when Christianna went through her nightly ablutions, she looked at her robe and reminded herself that she needed to be ready in case Joshua came. However, if he didn't come soon, it was all right. She could wait. No hurry. She had things under control. Besides, life was no longer boring or routine. Her times with Kosmos brought a new experience to each day.

It had been a long time since she had read Joshua's letters, but then she knew what they said anyway. At Kosmos' suggestion she was reading other parchments he had given her. After all, she wanted to realize her full potential. There was a whole world out there to learn about! If Joshua was as wealthy as she supposed, she needed to be equipped to meet that world. Why, she might even want to go into a little business on her own. Surely Joshua would admire that . . . or if he didn't, he should.

Relaxed now and comfortable, Christianna lost her anxiety over her relationship with Kosmos. She knew that he would love to have her as a wife, yet it seemed that he had resigned himself to simply being a friend. Christianna was thrilled. She so enjoyed his company. Therefore, it didn't bother her too much when occasionally, as they walked, he would reach over and take her hand in his. No one saw it. No one knew. And they both understood it could never be more than that. Besides, it felt good every now and then to hold a firm, masculine hand.

Then it happened. One day when they were out walking in their field of friendship—as they called it—a sudden deluge of rain burst forth. It was one of the first downpours of the early rainy season that came annually to their land. As the huge pelts of water began to attack them, they laughed and headed toward the hill.

"There is a cave up there we can use as a shelter until the storm passes," Christianna shouted above the wind. "Follow me." She dashed off, with Kosmos following.

When Christianna arrived at the mouth of the cave, she abruptly turned to yell at Kosmos to hurry, not realizing he was right behind her. As she turned, she knocked him off his feet. Reaching to help him catch his footing, she slipped on the smooth rock entrance to the cave, and both went tumbling to the ground. As they fell, Kosmos blocked Christianna's fall with his body so that she landed on top of him. By now both were soaking wet, and they began to laugh uproariously. Christianna's laughter was muffled as she buried her head in his chest.

Suddenly she realized that Kosmos was no longer laughing. He was motionless beneath her. Raising her head and pushing herself up from his chest, she looked into his face. Laughter had been replaced by passion. Embarrassed, she slid off him, never taking her eyes from his. Reaching up and removing the veil that hung to the side of her head, he grabbed her hair and brought her lips to his.

Christianna did not resist. She had been lured into a snare from which, for a moment, she did not want to escape. The bait was too sweet, too delicious to her taste. Little did she realize how bitter it would be in her stomach.

Christianna's friendship with Kosmos died . . . in adultery.

CHAPTER
TEN

*T*rumpets! *Startled awake, Christianna sat up in bed and listened carefully. No one was stirring. She ran out of her room, almost frantic to get to the roof. From there she could see all the way to the main road that led to their village. There weren't that many two-story homes to block her view. But she saw no lights, heard no singing, no shouts of rejoicing—no procession through the streets.*

For a number of nights now she had been awakened the same way. *I must have been dreaming again. But it's so real. Oh, God, what will I do when he does come? How can I bear to see him, to look at him?*

Christianna started back to her room. The dampness of the tile felt good against her feet. She longed to lie down and cool her face against the floor. But lest she wake her parents and cause all sorts of questions, she went to her room. She knew that she could not hold back the tears much longer.

They had seemed to be her food night and day. Fortunately her parents thought she was simply going through a period of depression after waiting so long to be claimed by her bridegroom.

As Christianna walked into her room, the light from her oil lamp illuminated the bright linen of her wedding robe. It had been almost two years since it had been completed, for she had been waiting almost three years now. Tomorrow would be the first Tishri, and the men of her village would be going to Jerusalem for the Festival of Tabernacles. When would she go to Jerusalem with her Joshua? When would the trumpet herald not the Feast of Trumpets and the Day of Atonement but the coming of her bridegroom?

She had sinned, and she knew it. She had experienced a grief almost unto death. Had it not been for Joshua's letters, had it not been for the assurance that he knew her inside and out and still loved her, had it not been for the certainty of his covenant, she would have despaired totally of life. Oh, how sustaining Joshua's letters had been! His words had become more precious than her necessary food. Now, day by day, moment by moment, she clung to his every word, his every promise. *I have to believe that Joshua is who and what he says he is. If he is not, then there is no pardon, no forgiveness . . . if he is not, then life holds nothing for me.* His words were her life! Without them she would have died by her own hand.

Christianna had not seen Kosmos since that day in the cave. She never wanted to see him again. The pleasure was over in a very short season, but she still wrestled constantly with the "whys." *Why did I not flee my youthful lusts? Why did I doubt Joshua's words? Why did I believe a lie? Why did I think I could be friends with one such as Kosmos and not come away contaminated!*

Yet for all this, Christianna was not bitter. Even though Kosmos had never even tried to see her again, she was not angry. She harbored no bitter feelings toward him. She realized he had achieved his goal. He had backed off, played it smart, waited until the time was right, and gotten what he wanted. But Kosmos had raped neither her nor her soul. After all, she had given in. She had not cried out for help. In a very real sense, he had used her for his pleasure alone—and she had let him. She acknowledged her sin. She accepted the responsibility for her actions.

"But you will neither destroy me nor keep me from Joshua. You will not triumph, Kosmos. I will prove you wrong about Joshua. Joshua loves me unconditionally." Although she was alone, she spoke the words aloud and with great determination. "Joshua said he would love me unconditionally. He promised me he would never forsake me no matter what. I will cling to his promises. I will not let you destroy me, and I will not take my life! Rather, I shall lay it down in a sacrifice of love at Joshua's feet." She would endure.

Yet there was one thing Christianna dreaded. What would she do when she saw Joshua? How . . . when would she tell him? *Oh, Joshua, Joshua, why, why did I do this to you? Against you and against my God have I sinned and done this awful thing in your sight. Oh, God, purge me. Purge me, and I shall be whiter than snow.*

God would purge her, she knew, but never would she stand under Joshua's *huppah* as a virgin. She had sown to the flesh, and of the flesh she had reaped corruption.

Christianna's mat was once again wet with tears. They were tears of sorrow that had led to a genuine repentance, but tears, she knew, that she would have never needed to shed had she only fled the day she met Kosmos. A deep sleep came. Then trumpets . . . again.

CHAPTER
ELEVEN

"**T**ishri, that's what it is, Tishri!" Christianna murmured as she rolled over onto her tummy. Her eyes still closed, she pulled the covering over her head. Her eyes felt swollen from crying, and she was not yet ready to face the brightness of the morning sun. Snuggling deep into her mat, she thought, If only they were Joshua's trumpets! The trumpets had blown twice, so Christianna knew it was not another one of her dreams. She had been awake for sure when she heard them the second time.

Sleep now eluded her, yet she felt rested. Flopping over onto her back, she stretched and decided to brave the morning light. As she stretched, once again she heard the sound of trumpets. They seemed even louder now.

Christianna opened her eyes. Why, it was pitch black! By now adrenalin was coursing through her veins, almost catapulting her from her bed. She flew through her door and up to the roof. The night air that greeted her was clear and crisp. The stars and moon shone brightly, undimmed by clouds.

Looking toward the road that led to their village, she saw in the distance what seemed to be a hundred little lights scattered out like the trail of a falling star. Then the sound of a trumpet pierced her heart.

"Joshua!" she cried. "Joshua, oh, Joshua, it's you! It's you!" Running back into the house, she was screaming with delight. "He's come! He's finally come! Joshua's coming!" She ran into her parents' room, almost knocking her mother over. "Father, Father, hurry! Get up! Put on your wedding garment!"

Bernice and Massah looked at one another. A smile of relief passed between them. They had been worried about their daughter. She had spent hours and hours alone in her room, reading and rereading Joshua's letters. Her bread had seemed to be the bread of sorrow. The daily puffiness of her eyes, swollen from crying, had been of great concern. But then Christianna had been waiting three years! What else could one expect? It seemed too long for any young virgin to wait, especially without ever seeing the one who was to be her bridegroom.

"Oh, Father, do you suppose our friends and relatives have heard the trumpets?"

"Yes, Christianna, yes. Do not worry, my child. You know that the men of the procession shall knock on the doors and call the people to come. And the women . . . you know women . . . they will run to the rooftops and spread the message like fire out of control. I bet you can hear them shouting even now." With that, Massah playfully cupped his hands over his mouth and, in a high-pitched, shrill imitation of a woman's voice, cried, "The voice of the bridegroom is in the streets! Behold, behold, the bridegroom cometh!" Amused with himself, he turned to Christianna. "Hurry! Run! Begin your preparations, or Joshua will be here and you will not be ready!"

As Christianna picked up her robe and ran from the room, her mother, who was almost as excited, shouted, "I will be right there, Christianna."

When Christianna reached the door of her room, she stopped abruptly. It hit her like a load of stone. *I'm going to see him. I'm going to see Joshua.* The words had to be said. They had to be shouted! And shout she did. "I'm going to see Joshua face to face! I'm going to see my bridegroom!" The joy of the moment had covered the grief of her transgression. Her garments of mourning had been changed for the oil of gladness.

Grabbing the vials of special perfumes and oils made for this day, Christianna began anointing her body. Looking into her mirror of highly polished silver, another gift from her bridegroom,

Christianna smoothed oil on her face and then began brushing her hair. It glimmered like the blackness of a raven's feathers. It would hang loose and flowing until she reached Joshua's home; then her maidens would braid it with pearls and gold.

As Christianna slipped on her wedding attire, she could hear the shouts of joy and mirth in the streets. Lyres, flutes, drums, and other musical instruments became heralds of the approaching bridegroom. The commotion was great. It seemed as if the whole village had turned out. Some of them were red of face as they were grabbed by dancers and whirled into the celebration amidst shouts of, "And you said Joshua, son of Shaddai, did not even exist. Here he is! Joshua! Look at him!"

And there he was . . . Joshua, son of Shaddai of the holy city Jerusalem. The scent of his flowing unseamed robe filled the streets with the rich odors of frankincense and myrrh. His girdle was not of the finest silk, brilliantly colored—it was of gold! Majesty and strength seemed to radiate from the tip of his magnificent gold crown to the toes of his feet, which were like burnished bronze carefully laced into luxuriously figured sandals. He not only looked like a king—he looked like a king of kings!

Mouths that had laughed or scorned or ridiculed, mouths that had belittled Christianna's person, Joshua's existence, or the reality of their betrothal were suddenly closed. Strangely, they suddenly remembered and felt accountable for what they had said. Yet they did not run and hide. They could not. They seemed paralyzed by awe.

Those who had refused wedding garments now wanted to be included in the festivities. Some ran from one to the other crying, "Sell me your wedding garment." Yet none would sell his garment, not for any price. This was one wedding they did not want to miss, and they knew that the ruler of the feast would never let anyone in without a wedding garment.

Those who had asked to be excused were sick with grief, for their excuses now took on a flimsy shabbiness in the light of the event before them.

Those without torches or lamps ran in frustration to seek to buy oil in order that they might join the wedding procession that was leaving Christianna's home for Jerusalem. Never, never had Christianna's village seen a wedding procession like this! A whole host of men had come with the bridegroom from Jerusalem. The streets were jammed, and they echoed with shouts of joy. It even seemed as if the distant mountains were singing and as if the trees were clapping their hands for joy.

By the time the wedding procession reached the house of Massah, the house was full of excited relatives and intimate friends. Oohs, ahhs, and other exclamations of awe and appreciation were heard as Christianna stepped into the courtyard. There she stood, clothed in fine linen, bright and clean, a crown of gold upon her head. Wrinkled fingers, which had checked out many a wedding robe, stroked the fine bright linen of her garment, and heads nodded approvingly. Then the oldest of women spoke. "Christianna, you are prepared as a bride adorned for her husband."

The moment had come! Amidst shouts of joy and the music of a multitude of stringed instruments, the door of Christianna's home was flung open and Joshua stepped across the threshold.

"Joshua." Christianna's whisper of reverence and awe was heard by all; and, as in the days of Joshua of old, the sun, moon, and stars seemed to stand still. Seeing Joshua was like taking a step into eternity where time matters no more. In a courtyard full of people, the two were alone. When Joshua spoke, his voice was like the sound of many waters.

"How beautiful you are, my darling. How beautiful you are! Your eyes are like doves."

Christianna's eyes never left his, and they never wanted to. Never in all her life had she seen such eyes . . . they were untainted, as if they had never beheld anything unholy or impure. No hint of lust, greed, sensuality, or even pride desecrated them. Rather, they seemed to be deep, rich pools of love surrounded by majesty and strength. Without shame they caressed her, held her, adored her. His look made her feel a security she had never even fathomed possible.

Christianna's eyes never left Joshua's as she said, "How handsome you are, my beloved. And so pleasant. My beloved is like a gazelle or a young stag. Behold, he is standing within our walls."

With that, Joshua held out his hands, and Christianna walked forward until they touched and her fingers were covered by his. Then Joshua said, "No one shall ever pluck you out of my hands." To which Christianna replied, "I am my beloved's, and he is mine. His desire is toward me."

Then her beloved responded and said to her, "Arise, my darling, my beautiful one, and come along. A place which I have prepared awaits you alone."

They left the house amidst shouts of blessing as Christianna's relatives called out, "Thou art our sister. Be thou the mother of thousands of millions, and let thy seed possess the gate of those who hate them."

CHAPTER TWELVE

The journey to Jerusalem was a joyous one. The bridesmaids, who had joined the wedding procession after Joshua had taken Christianna from her home, could not stop chattering over the magnificence of it all. Why, Joshua had even brought a beautiful traveling couch for Christianna. Sixty mighty men of Israel armed with swords surrounded it. Oh, how they loved that!

As Christianna, seated on her magnificent couch, took in the panorama of it all, the agony of her three years of waiting seemed as nothing in comparison to the glory of this one single event! Truly it was exceedingly abundantly above all she could ask or think, just as Joshua had promised.

Then, for one flashing moment, Christianna remembered Kosmos' eyes. They became cesspools, underground sewers that had sought to drown her, as they had countless others, in the lust of their own passions. Now Christianna could see. It was the difference between darkness and light, death and life, hell and heaven. Riding on her bridal couch, preceded by her husband, guarded by his armed host, headed for a place prepared just for her, Christianna knew that it was for this purpose that she had been born: to be the wife of Joshua, son of Shaddai.

The magnificence of Shaddai's home would have literally overwhelmed Christianna had she not been swept up and carried to a waiting chamber, filled with women who were anxious to see that she was refreshed from her journey. Some brought her drinks and dainties. Others brought forth more perfumed oils and spices. Then they began the task of braiding her hair with her exquisitely woven strands of pearls and gold. When all was done, her locks were then hidden beneath a thick veil.

As Christianna rose to follow them, she stopped so abruptly that they almost left her in the room. Suddenly realizing they were minus the bride, the women turned, almost in unison, and looked at her as if directed by some unseen hand. It made Christianna laugh.

"I pray thee, forgive me," she said. "It's just that I'm lovesick." That was all she could honestly claim.

Being the bride of Joshua was all grace—pure unmerited favor!

They loved her candid vulnerability. No pride. No shame. No pretense. No airs about this bride! They saw her poverty of spirit, and they approved.

They led Christianna to a palatial banquet hall illumined by some unseen brilliance. There, although she was surrounded by magnificent walls of gold and precious stone, she was the center of attention. All eyes were upon her as she joined her husband under the *huppah*.

Before sitting down and beginning the feast, Christianna looked at Joshua and said, "Like an apple tree among the trees of forest, so is my beloved among the young men. In your shade I take great delight and sit down, and your fruit is sweet to my taste. You have brought me, Christianna, your bride, to your banqueting hall, and your *huppah* over me is love. Sustain me with raisin cakes and refresh me with apples because I am lovesick. Let your left hand be under my head and your right hand embrace me."

The festivities went on for hours. After the governor of the feast returned thanks and blessed the wine, one after another the guests arose to give benedictions to Joshua and Christianna. Riddle after riddle interspersed the benedictions. Gaiety and joy prevailed. But none, besides the bride and groom, was more fulfilled than Shaddai.

Shaddai looked at Joshua and Christianna and was satisfied. Totally, completely, absolutely satisfied! Joshua had his bride! His family was complete. *Well, complete except for Rachel*, Shaddai thought. *And someday, Rachel, my faithless wife, you shall return. Oh, Rachel, Rachel, how oft would I have gathered you as a hen gathers her chicks, but you would not come to me.*

The years had been so painful for Joshua and Shaddai. Time and time again Shaddai had pled with Rachel to return to him, but to no avail.

Like Christianna, Rachel had been nothing before Shaddai found her. Unwashed and naked, her navel cord uncut, she was an infant who had been abandoned in an open field. Shaddai had rescued her and watched her grow into womanhood. Then he had entered into a covenant with her, and Rachel became his wife. Nothing was too good for her! She was dressed in the finest linen and embroidered cloth, adorned with ornaments of gold and silver. Shaddai adored her, and Rachel adored him, following wherever he led.

Shaddai could not help but sigh as he looked at the bridal couple. It reminded him of Rachel's early devotion. But her devotion had begun to wane as the fame of her beauty was spread abroad. Caught up with her own beauty and the admiration of men, she gave herself to those who were merely passers-by, taking the beautiful clothes and ornaments her husband had given her and using them for her harlotries.

Time had not healed Shaddai's hurt, but he blinked back the tears. Now was no time for tears. This was a day of rejoicing, a day that he and Joshua had long awaited. Although Rachel was not there to share it, he was confident that one day she would be his again. In fact, he had recently heard that she was to be sold as a slave, and his plans were already made. He would buy her out of slavery, forgive her, and restore her to her rightful place at his side. That would prove his unconditional love!

Rachel might not know or understand herself, but Shaddai did. He knew she would return to him, trembling at his goodness. Once again she would be his and his alone. *Oh, Joshua, Joshua,* Shaddai thought. *What a day of celebration that shall be! Then all will be complete—just as I have planned, just as we have purposed. It shall all come to pass in the fullness of time.*

At that moment, Joshua caught his father's eye and winked at him. As Joshua nodded his head toward Christianna, his finger pointed back and forth from Christianna on her throne to himself on his throne and then to Shaddai and the empty throne beside him. Shaddai nodded almost imperceptibly and smiled. He knew his son was aware of his thoughts about his mother. Both were confident that Rachel would return to them. Once again, Shaddai thought back on the last few weeks when Rachel had been the topic of much discussion. As Joshua had prepared his quarters for Christianna's homecoming, Shaddai could not help but think of Rachel and the time of their betrothal, and he had needed to talk. How thankful this father and son were for each other. It had made the years of waiting for their wives more tolerable.

Shaddai also remembered how anxious his son had been to go for his bride. Yet as a father, he had to make sure that all was totally prepared before he could give him leave to go.

"Everything in its proper time, my son," Shaddai had said. "Christianna needs this time of preparation, this time of consecration. After all, she will rule with you over all that I own. She must be set apart so that she might learn how to rule and reign as befits the wife of Joshua, the daughter of Shaddai. She is destined for a throne. Your mother did not learn. She forgot where she came from, who she was, and her heart was lifted up. This cannot happen to Christianna. She must be tried, tested . . . never more than she can bear, but tested she must be."

At times when Shaddai had talked like this, Joshua had interceded on Christianna's behalf. "But, Father, what if she falls? What if she stumbles? What if her love for me wanes? After all, it's hard, Father. I know. It's hard on me. Besides, she has never seen me. The only contact we've had is through my letters and Eliezer!"

"Son, my son . . . I pray she does not fall. But if she does, the question is, will she stay down or will she repent? If she stumbles, she'll get up. She'll repent. I know, Son. Trust me."

"Father, I believe you . . . but, oh, please let me go for her soon."

Shaddai shook his head. He would never forget the day when he had walked into Joshua's quarters, looked at them, and said, "Perfect! Magnificent! Fit for a bride adorned for her husband. Go, quickly, Son. Christianna is ready. She's waiting!"

Now his family was complete. Finally, all that he and Joshua had planned had come to pass in the fullness of time. Eternity stretched before them . . . and it was theirs to enjoy.

Sensing it was time to remove the *huppah* to Joshua's bridal chamber, Shaddai called to his servants, "After I give the blessing, take the banner and put it over Joshua's couch."

Joshua had been watching his father carefully, for Shaddai was still his model in all things. Seeing him rise, Joshua knew it was time for him and Christianna to receive Shaddai's blessing.

As they stood side by side, Shaddai began: "This is my beloved son with whom I am well pleased. He has glorified me here on this earth with the glory I have given him. Never has he failed to manifest to all that for which my name stands. I, therefore, do hereby exalt him with a name above every name, that the homage given to me might also be given to him."

Then he turned to his beloved daughter.

"Christianna, may you and Joshua be one, even as Joshua and I are one, thee in him and he in thee. May you be forever perfected in unity. All that is mine is now yours. Together you are joint heirs. Joshua and I have loved you with an everlasting love, and with lovingkindness we have bought you. You are ours, and we are yours. Our love shall be in you forever."

CHAPTER
THIRTEEN

*C*hristianna stood all alone in the bridal chamber, *waiting for Joshua. The betrothal was about to be consummated. She looked at their bed, covered with silks. No cloths of virginity lay upon it, for Joshua had forbidden them. Yet had he called for them, it would have been useless, she thought. Her heart pounded within her.*

The smell of exotic spices and perfumes permeated the coverings. Above the bed was the *huppah*, the same banner they had eaten under during the marriage feast. Magnificent seemed such an inadequate word to describe all that her eyes could take in. It was a word that seemed small, dwarfed in the presence of such opulence and grandeur. Yet at that moment, Christianna would have sold it all, everything but Joshua, in exchange for one thing. Oh, if only she could give Joshua the gift of her virginity.

Oh, my anguish, my anguish! I writhe in pain. This is my punishment, and oh, God, how bitter it is! How it pierces my heart. Oh, Joshua, Joshua, my beloved, you do not even know.

There were no tears now. The tears had been replaced by an agony of heart too deep for tears, an agony that made her hurt so badly that she was void of emotion. No tears could be pain's solace, pain's balm of Gilead.

In a moment, all would be naked and open to his sight, and Christianna knew she would have to give an account of the things she had done with her body.

Oh, Adonai, it is no longer myself that I am concerned about. It is Joshua! Oh, Lord God, how, how can I ever tell him that I failed to love him with all my heart, with all my mind, with all my soul, with all my strength . . . with all my body?

The door to the bridal chamber opened just as Christianna slipped into her gown of silk. As Joshua walked across the room, her eyes could not get their fill of him.

Oh, Joshua, she thought, *magnificent, wonderful, glorious perfection. How could I have ever settled for less? How could I have given myself to a devil when a god was mine?*

Cupping her face in his hands, he looked at her with complete love, and delight filled his voice. "You are altogether beautiful, my darling, and there is no blemish in you." Joshua's words made her wince, like a sword through her heart. Then he lifted her into his arms, and she leaned her head against his all-sufficient chest. *Maybe he will never know, maybe I can hide it.*

As Joshua carried Christianna across the room, he whispered in her ear, "Come with me, my bride, you have made my heart beat faster. My sister, my bride, you have made my heart beat faster with a single glance of your eyes, with a single strand of your necklace." Gently he laid her under the banner, and as he stood back to look at her, pure delight enveloped him. "How beautiful is your love, my sister, my bride. How much better is your love than wine, and the fragrance of your oils than all kinds of spices!"

Then Joshua leaned down and, for the first time, kissed her. Heaven and earth fled away. They were caught in eternity. "Your lips, my bride, drip honey; honey and milk are under your tongue, and the fragrance of your garments is like the fragrance of Lebanon."

His eyes caressed her, taking in the essence of her beauty. As his lips brushed across her face, Joshua entreated her as he whispered in her ear, "A garden locked is my sister, my bride, a rock garden locked, a spring sealed up." He paused. "May I come into my garden and eat its choice fruits?"

She knew he waited for permission. *Oh, Joshua,* Christianna thought, *all you want is what pleases me.*

My pleasure is your utmost concern. How different you are from the one who ravished your garden for his own pleasure. The thought brought pain. Excruciating pain. Christianna closed her eyes and bit her lip, but still she could not hold back the sob that came from the very wellspring of her heart.

In an instant, Joshua was on his knees beside the bed. Placing both hands under her back, he drew her to his breast. "Oh, Christianna, Christianna, I'm sorry, my beloved. So sorry," he said as he tenderly rocked her back and forth.

Christianna sobbed and sobbed convulsively until finally she was spent. Loosening her grip, she lay limp in his arms. His back was red and sore where she had dug her nails into his flesh. When Joshua spoke, his voice was choked. "I love you, my darling, my sister, my bride. I love you. Here sit up, look at me, my dove."

Until now, Christianna had not said a word. Sitting on the edge of the bed, she reached out to caress the face of the man who knelt on the floor before her. "Joshua, oh, Joshua, how I have longed for this day, for this moment. I love you, Joshua. I love you now more than I ever loved you. I love you more than life itself."

"Christianna."

"Oh, Joshua," she cried, dropping her head, "I've—" Joshua put his hand to her lips.

"Christianna! Christianna, look at me. I know you love me." His words were spoken deliberately, encased in conviction. "And I love you unconditionally. You are bone of my bone, flesh of my flesh. Nothing . . . nothing in your past, nothing in your future . . . nothing now shall ever quench my love for you."

Then, looking her straight in the eyes, Joshua said, "I love you with an everlasting love. I understand your anguish; I hurt with you. I only wish, Christianna, for your sake, my beloved, that you had waited."

Many waters cannot quench love,
Nor will rivers overflow it.
If a man were to give all the riches
of his house for love,
It would be utterly despised.
Behold,
I have loved you
with an everlasting love.

EPILOGUE

"I only wish, Christianna, for your sake, that you had waited."

Beloved Christians, someday soon the trumpet shall suddenly sound (1 Thessalonians 4:15-17), and your Heavenly Bridegroom, the Lord Jesus Christ, shall come to take you to His Father's home (John 14:2-3).

Oh, I realize that sometimes you grow weary of waiting and that sometimes you wonder, "Where is the promise of His coming?" (2 Peter 3:1-4). Yet you can be sure that this same Jesus, who has been taken up from you into heaven, will come again for those who eagerly await Him (Acts 1:11; Hebrews 9:28). And when He comes, the mouths of those who mocked and scorned will be stopped, and those who excused themselves and refused to come to the wedding will be speechless (Romans 3:19; 1:20; Matthew 22:1-14). There will be many who will find themselves shut out because they were not prepared for His coming (Matthew 25:1-13). They will have believed a lie from the father of lies, the prince of this world, the one who had them walk according to the course of this *kosmos*, and who, if he could, would have kept your eyes blind to the glorious truth about the Lover of your soul (John 8:44; 14:30; Ephesians 2:2; 2 Corinthians 4:4).

But, praise God, your El Shaddai is rich in mercy, and, because of the great love with which He has loved you (Ephesians 2:4), He has, by His grace (Ephesians 2:5), called you, "Beloved," when there was nothing lovely about you (Romans 9:25). He called you when you were foolish, weak, base, and despised, and He gave you to His Son, putting a new heart within you so that you will never turn away from Him (Ezekiel 36:26; Jeremiah 32:40). In Him alone can you boast (1 Corinthians 1:26-31). You, who were afar off, a stranger, an alien (Ephesians 2:11-22), an enemy of God (Romans 5:10), were chosen by Him (John 15:16) and betrothed (2 Corinthians 11:2) to His only begotten Son (John 3:16), to be the bride of Christ (Ephesians 5:25-32). As Christ's bride, God has given you His glory and made you one with Him (John 17:21-22).

And how did you come into this marvelous marriage of love? Through His Word, His Logos. God has written you letter after letter and has delivered them to you by His Spirit, who has revealed to you the things that would be freely

given you (1 Corinthians 2:9-13) if you would only
receive Him as your Lord (Romans 10:8-13).

Even as Abraham sent out his servant Eliezer
(Genesis 15:2) to find a bride for Isaac (Genesis 24),
so God drew you by His Spirit to His Son (John 6:44;
1 Corinthians 12:13) that you might become bone of
His bone and flesh of His flesh (Genesis 2:23;
Ephesians 5:31), never to be forsaken (Hebrews
13:5), never to be plucked from His hand (John
10:28-29), but to become an heir of God, a joint heir
with Christ (Romans 8:17).

Oh, the marriage is sure, but the consummation
of that marriage covenant is yet to come. And
though you have not seen your Joshua, your Jesus,
still you love Him (1 Peter 1:8) and await His coming
(1 Thessalonians 1:10), preparing your bridal robe
(Revelation 19:8).

And what will it be like on that day, when you
see Him face to face (1 John 3:2-3), when finally the
marriage is consummated (Revelation 19:7)? Shall
you be presented to Jesus Christ as a chaste virgin
(2 Corinthians 11:2) clothed in fine linen, bright and
clean because of your righteous acts (Revelation
19:8)? Or will you shrink back in shame at His
coming (1 John 2:28) because you have played the
adulteress with this world, this *kosmos* (James 4:4)?
Have you realized that, although He loves you with
an unconditional, everlasting love, still He jealously
desires you for Himself and Himself alone (James
4:5)?

Oh, beloved Christian, Christianna, this book is a plea, a plea to the bride, the body of Jesus Christ, to purify herself even as He is pure. The world is so enticing, so seductive, and it offers much temporal pleasure. But remember that it is temporal (2 Corinthians 4:18; 2 Peter 3:10-11). The pleasures of sin endure but for a season (Hebrews 11:25). When the devil can convince us that we do not need to be dependent upon God, when Satan lies to us and we begin to doubt the reality of the love of the Father and Son, when we listen to the world's siren song and grow weary of reading His letters, then we are vulnerable to the world's seduction. First we find ourselves spotted, stained with the world (James 1:27), then friends with the world (James 4:4), then entangled with the world (2 Timothy 2:4), then loving the world (1 John 2:15), until finally the inevitable follows, and we commit adultery . . . adultery with the enemy of God (James 4:4).

Has not our El Shaddai, God the Father, been hurt enough by the adulterous ways of His wife, Israel (Ezekiel 6:9), as over and over she played the harlot on every high hill and under every green tree (Jeremiah 3:6)? Will we now follow Israel's ways and bring grief upon grief to the Father as He watches His Son's wife consort with the world?

The world and its lusts, Christianna, are passing away (1 John 2:17). Your Joshua, Jesus Christ, has written: "Behold, I am coming quickly, and My reward is with Me, to render to every man according to what he has done" (Revelation 22:12).

What will it be like when the trumpet sounds and your Heavenly Bridegroom comes to take you for Himself, when the King brings you into His chambers (Song of Solomon 1:4)?

Remember, He loves you with an everlasting love (Jeremiah 31:3).

"Be thou faithful unto death" (Revelation 2:10).

*It is our prayer that God
will use this book to minister to you
in a personal way.*

Precept Ministries is a year-round
Bible study and conference center
dedicated to establishing
God's people in God's Word.
If you would like to
know more about
Kay Arthur or Precept Ministries,
please write or call:

Precept Ministries
P.O. Box 182218
Chattanooga, TN 37422-7218
(615) 892-6814

Also by Kay Arthur

How to Study Your Bible
Beloved
His Imprint, My Expression
God, Are You There?
Lord, Teach Me to Pray in 28 Days

International Inductive Study Series
The Call to Follow Jesus
Choosing Victory, Overcoming Defeat
Free From Bondage God's Way
God's Answers to Relationships and Passions
The Holy Spirit Unleashed in You
Teach Me Your Ways